Ethel Holliste. ⌐ ⌐⌐⌐⌐⌐⌐ Summer as a Campfire Girl

Irene Elliott Benson

Ethel Hollister's Second Summer As A Campfire Girl

CHAPTER I

ETHEL'S PLANS

The morning after Ethel had declared herself her mother came up to her room. She could see that Mrs. Hollister had not slept and her eyes were red from weeping. Ethel kissed her, saying:

"Mamma, we are going to be very happy together — you and I. I don't want to disappoint you, dear, nor would I do so willingly; but I simply can not live as I've been living. Sit down and let us talk."

Then she told of Aunt Susan, — of her kindness, unselfishness and self-sacrifice. She told of Mattie and how they had helped her, and of her Uncle John; of Patty and Judge Sands; and lastly of Kate and what a wonderful character she was.

"Wait, dear, I want to show you my ceremonial gown," and she quickly slipped it on. The girl's hair was still hanging unbound, having slept in it that way, and she hooked about it her coronation band. Said her mother:

"Well, I must say it is becoming. What a Pocahontas you would make in private theatricals!" she exclaimed with maternal pride; "But then, why should I speak of theatricals? You've given up all such things."

"Why, Mamma," laughed Ethel, "I'm not going into a convent. I have given up nothing but the unreal part of life."

"I suppose you'll tell everyone how poor we are, and how I have put you forward under false colors. Then people will despise me."

"No, Mamma, I shall not do a thing to put you in any awkward position. Keep on. Give your teas for me if you wish, — even have the two extra maids. It costs very little and we have a social time; it cheers Grandmamma and there's no need to stop them. But this is what I shall not do: First I shall tell Harvey Bigelow that Aunt Susan was once a millionaire but that she lost all of her money. I shall tell of her wonderful gifts to Akron, — of her charities, and how well she is beloved, but that I shall inherit no money from her. Harvey will tell his mother and she'll spread the news. If people care any the less for us after hearing it, let them go; but I don't propose to tell what Papa's salary is, or that you—poor dear—sit until morning sewing for me,—a thing that I'm not going to allow you to do any longer.

"Then I shall give up attending Madam's. Yes, don't start. Every bill Papa pays is a nail in his coffin, I know. Tomorrow I shall go to Barnard and try to pass an examination, and for one quarter what Madam charges I can get a sound and solid education, and were Papa to die I can leave with my teacher's diploma knowing something that will be of use to me. I could help support you and Grandmamma. What could I do were I forced to support myself after leaving Madam's. Why, an education such as her girls receive is of no earthly account unless for music or such accomplishments; but with a degree from Barnard I can earn good money. I am so glad that I am young and that I shall have a chance. You'll be proud of me, Mamma,— just wait and see," and she kissed her mother affectionately.

They went down to breakfast. Archibald Hollister listened to his daughter's plans. He was proud of her and his face showed it.

"You see, Papa," continued Ethel, "every penny is spent on me. Do you and Mamma ever go to a theatre? No. Do you ever take a drive? Never,—why? Because you can't spare the money. Now at least we shall be able to go to the moving picture shows and take Grandmamma. I bet you'd enjoy it, wouldn't you, Grandmamma? And, do you know, the best people go, and a quarter is the highest priced seat."

The girl chatted on until the postman delivered the mail.

"Oh! a letter from Kate. Let's see what news she has written," and she gave a gasp as she read the first page.

"Poor Mrs. Casey died Saturday from pneumonia. Nora is heartbroken, and poor Pat Casey acts as though he knew not which way to turn. Nora looks really refined in black,—almost handsome. She loved Mrs. Casey, who in spite of her peculiarities was a good wife and mother. Later: Mr. Casey wishes to take Nora away. He suggested New York, so you may see her, etc."

Then Ethel described Honora.

"It is strange but I can never like that girl. There's something about her that's antagonistic to me, and yet when she comes here I must be polite and ask her to visit me."

"If she's in mourning she'll not expect to meet people," said Mrs.

Hollister quickly, "nor to go to any places of amusement, thank heavens."

"Oh, she's very generous. Probably she'd invite us, Mamma. Well, poor

Nora, she loved her mother. I'm sorry for her."

CHAPTER II

ETHEL ENTERS COLLEGE

The next morning Ethel Hollister walked up to Barnard and put in her application for admittance. The following week upon her first examination she failed, but she entered the class with conditions. The girl studied hard and soon made good.

She liked the girls of her class. They were intelligent, athletic, and agreeable.

Her former friends and companions from La Rue's declared that of late — in fact, since she had become a Camp Fire Girl — Ethel Hollister had developed fads. This Barnard was one. But as Ethel kept on steadily progressing in college, and she was so very young — not yet seventeen — people began to consider her a girl of great ability and intelligence. Mrs. Hollister grew to be proud of hearing her praised on every side and Archibald seemed less worried over money matters. She was rather glad that things had changed. Perhaps it was all for the best, and people would respect them no less.

Grandmother never wearied of hearing her grandchild tell of her visit. "And to think," she'd say, "that Susan has had all the trouble she tells of and has made no sign. How gladly would I have helped her. Still, had I done so we would have had no house. Well, the Lord knows what's best. We could only have offered her a home. I'm glad the Insane Asylum was endowed and the boys educated before the crash came."

Nora did not visit New York in the winter. She went South with her father. The girls — Kate and Ethel — corresponded, and in that way Ethel heard all of the news. The Judge came often and took Patty and Kate on long motor trips. Mattie was doing nicely. She was employed in a Woman's Exchange where she received twelve dollars a week and taught cooking and sewing. Mollie was improving daily. Mr. Hastings had a fine position with Judge Sands. Honora was away, but the rest of the girls were as usual. The Camp

5

Fires met weekly and everyone missed Ethel, but no one missed her as did Aunt Susan. "Why," wrote Kate, "she says the light has gone out of her life, and Tom roams around disconsolate. But," she added, "you should see the up-to-date way in which he dresses. He is the pink of fashion, I tell you."

Ethel laughed, and while reading would stop every now and then to explain.

Then Ethel answered:

"I have joined Miss Westcott's Camp Fire Girls, and if you believe it, Mamma goes with me. She doesn't like it, but she's a great help to me and to the girls, for she teaches them so much. She's consistent and it will take her some time to overcome her prejudices. Nanny Bigelow belongs, and Harvey takes us when Mamma can not go. By the way, Harvey seems quite interested in medicine, and after graduating he is going to study it. We call him 'Doctor' Bigelow.

"Dorothy Kip's Day Nursery has proved a great success. It is the dearest little flat, and the babies are sweet. Dorothy's old woman is a great help, and I want you to know that Dorothy works hard. Why, she almost runs the place on contributions and her allowance, and the little ones are just as happy and comfortable as possible. She has books and toys, and we girls take turns in going in and reading to the elder children, as well as amusing the younger ones. That is a good charity, and Grandmother (Kate noticed that Ethel had begun to call Mrs. Hollister 'Mother' and the old lady 'Grandmother') goes nearly every pleasant day and takes flowers. She generally spends the afternoon with them, so in a small way Dorothy Kip is emulating Jane Addams. Who knows but some day she may be her equal,—Oh!"

The second letter said:

"I must tell you something. The other evening Harvey Bigelow called. You know I never liked him any more than I liked Mattie nor Nora. Now I like Mattie and I am beginning to like Harvey. I hope I shall change towards

Nora, but I see no sign now. Well, Harvey began.

"'Miss Ethel,' he said, 'I've determined to become a physician. I presume you've heard that, and I'm determined to become a good one, too. You may not know it, but I have always liked boys. I don't say that I dislike girls, — but I do like boys. (Harvey is developing a sense of humor.) When I visited my college chum—Joe Atkinson—this last summer, I was surprised to learn that he was the Scout Master to a troop of eight boys. He lives in Springfield, Illinois. I had a corking visit and a fine time with the kids, two of whom are his young brothers.

"'Do you know, I became mightily interested in the movement. I have studied and watched it and I think it's the finest thing ever started. I came home quite enthusiastic and I talked of it to the two younger Kip boys and Alan McAllister,—Grace's brother. If you'll believe it, before I realized what I'd done, these boys had formed a troop and began to importune me to be the Scout Master of it. There's the two Kips, Tom Wilder (Sara Judson's cousin), a brother of Grace McAllister, Tommy Westcott, and my cousin, Jack Atwater, besides two other boys from the East Side Y.M.C.A. Miss Westcott, the Guardian of the Camp Fire Girls, asked that they might be allowed to join, making eight in all.'

"I caught him by the hand and I said:

"'Harvey Bigelow, I take off my hat to you. I never liked you so well in my life."

"He blushed awfully and seemed embarrassed, but he simply said:

"'Don't you think it about time that I became in earnest over something in life? The opportunity presented itself and I grasped it—that's all.'

"Well, to make a long story short, several of these boys are desirous of going West next summer and spending their vacations instead of East, and he called to ask me about the Muskingum Camp. He is going there, Kate, and he'll be near us. I made him write to Mr. Adams—your father's man— who did everything for us, and ask him to reserve a place for the Scouts.

7

I'm just wild for summer to come. I'm going to bring Mother and Grandmother. Grandmother will visit Aunt Susan, and Mother can spend her time between Aunt Susan's, your house, and the Camp. She doesn't say much but I really think the change is a relief to her—poor dear little mother. I was the selfish juggernaut who made her sacrifice everyone for me. I realize it now, and thank God it's not too late to mend.

"I am doing finely at college. I should like to form from some of my class another Company of Camp Fire Girls, but the trouble is they are too busy with study. They say that they're worn out when summer comes and have to go away to rest, but they intend to join during their third year. Then it won't be such a continuous grind as it is now.

"I am so glad that I had the good sense to start in college. I intend to be self-supporting after I graduate. I consider it a glorious thing for an unmarried woman—don't you?

"Well, dear, I must close. Kiss Uncle John, etc."

That was great news for Kate—that Harvey Bigelow should have become a man. It was too good to be true. She sent the letter to Aunt Susan, whom she knew would be interested in it.

"I tell you, Ethel is made of good stuff!" ejaculated Uncle John. "She was in the right church but in the wrong pew—that's all."

CHAPTER III

ETHEL AND HARVEY BECOME FIRM FRIENDS

Vacation arrived. Ethel had acquitted herself well, and her examinations were excellent. She and her mother began making preparations to go West.

This time it was Grandmother and Mrs. Hollister whose wardrobes needed replenishing. Ethel bought for herself two new suits and some blouses. She had actually outgrown hers of the preceding summer.

"My dear, I am spending very little money now," said Mrs. Hollister, "and I'm going to put some by for your trousseau."

Ethel laughed merrily.

"Why, Mother, where's the man?"

"Never mind," replied her mother, "he'll come."

"Mother, you're a born matchmaker!" exclaimed the girl. "I wish you had had other daughters."

"Heaven forbid!" ejaculated Mrs. Hollister with a funny little smile.

"One is enough."

"Is that intended for a compliment?" laughed the girl. "If so it's a doubtful one."

During the month of May, Harvey would invite her to go horseback riding up to Van Cortlandt Park. They had to make it Saturdays, as that was Ethel's only free day. They usually started early. On the country roads the apple and peach blossoms were like pictures. To the girl they brought back the previous spring at Aunt Susan's, and especially the morning when she had revealed to Ethel the sad story of her married life. On one of these excursions the girl related it to Harvey.

"By George!" he ejaculated when she had finished, "that old lady is a sport and no mistake. She's all right. I imagined she was made of different stuff from other women, and do you know I sort of suspected that she hadn't all the money that your mother thought she had. She was too refined and showed good blood. Had she been so wealthy, from her dressing people might have taken her for a miser, and gentle folks are seldom misers. I thought that it was necessity that caused her to wear those old-fashioned clothes, so I argued that though Mrs. Hollister imagined her wealthy and that you were in a line to inherit her money there was a great mistake somewhere. But pshaw! as for that every mother is ambitious for her daughter. Why, my mother left no stone unturned until she had married Edith to Lord Ashurst, and I must admit that I was easily led by my mother. Why, I've been out for a rich wife ever since I left school; but, Ethel, I've changed. Now I propose to pay my bills with the money I earn, not with hers; nor shall I allow her to buy what she wears."

"Does your mother realize how you feel?" asked Ethel, pushing her fair, curling locks from her eyes.

"Bless you, yes. She and I had one long talk, and after it I tell you there was something doing in the Bigelow family; but Nannie who has lots of horse sense sided with me, and together we were too many for mother. She saw that it was up to her to make the best of it and she did, but like your mother she still cherishes her ambitions. Nan said to her:

"'You have one daughter who has done the grand marriage stunt and she's some class. Do let us choose for ourselves."

"What did your mother say to that?" laughed Ethel.

"I think she boxed Nannie's ears and then apologized. She loses her self-control sometimes. Poor mother," and Harvey laughed. "Nannie has some temper, too, and don't you make any mistake."

Ethel was beginning to have a real friendly feeling for Harvey. He asked many questions about her cousin Kate.

"She rings true," he said. "I liked her from the first."

"She is true," replied Ethel. "You'll see her this summer, and I'm sure you'll like Uncle John and his wife. He's just a dear."

Those were red letter days for Ethel. She enjoyed the air, the scenery, and the rides; and she enjoyed talking to Harvey, for now that he understood she could talk to him as though he were one of the family—without restriction and without embarrassment.

"What puzzles me," said Ethel, "is the way our mothers argue. When they plan our marriages it's only money and position. Love never seems to enter into their heads. Oh! I grew so tired of it. Thank God it's over, and our family are now normal. Even Grandmother wished me to marry well. I had far rather be an old maid than to be tied to a man for whom I care nothing, and have to sit opposite and pour tea for him three hundred and sixty-five days in a year. Imagine the horrible monotony of that. I heard that advice given to a girl in a play and I never forgot it; and if only girls could be brought to realize beforehand the sin of it there would be fewer unhappy marriages."

CHAPTER IV
ETHEL'S SECOND TRIP

The time arrived for the Hollisters to start. There were tears in Archibald Hollister's eyes as he kissed them goodbye at the train. Within the last year his life had been happier. He had seen more of his wife and had grown to love her better than he had since Ethel was a child. She and he were together nearly all of the time, and it was like reading over a forgotten love story.

"Don't you worry, papa," said Ethel, patting his cheek. "We're going to keep well and have a lovely summer, and when you come up for your vacation you'll be like a boy again."

"Yes, Archie," spoke up Mrs. Hollister "Be sure that Mirinda gives you good things to eat and has them well cooked. She'll have little else to do, and you go out and call on the Bigelows and Judsons. Take in the moving pictures and roof gardens. I'll trust you," she laughed, "but don't fail to write me three times a week, will you, telling me how things are going on. And don't let Mirinda's young man come to the house but once a week and on Sundays."

"Remember everything," laughed Ethel.

Grandmother kissed her son and murmured:

"God bless you, Archie. I expect to take on a new lease of life."

"Do mother," said the man, "we all need you."

The trip was pleasant. The scenery was fine and the country looked as though it had been freshly swept and dusted, everything seemed so clean. Grandmother's eyes glistened with pleasure. They were to stop at Akron first, where they were to leave Grandmother, and after a visit of a week Ethel and her mother were to go on to Columbus and hence to Camp.

As the train drew into the depot at Akron, there stood Tom with Aunt Susan, but what a metamorphosis! Tom just escaped being a fashionably dressed swell. He was too manly for that. He wore a blue serge suit, colored negligee shirt with tie to match, a Panama hat, and russet ties. His handsome face was so full of character that Mrs. Hollister whispered to Ethel:

"What a remarkably distinguished looking man he is. You never told me of his being so."

Ethel blushed when Tom took her up and kissed her as he might have done had she been his sister, and as for Aunt Susan, even Grandmother gazed at her with amazement. She was attired in a modish little automobile bonnet, close fitting and of grey, while her grey linen suit gave her an up-to-date air, for now, she proudly informed Ethel, Tom owned his own car.

"Aunt Susan, you look out of sight," said Ethel, kissing her. "I never knew you."

Mrs. Hollister was happy. Ethel had not half told her, and she was agreeably disappointed. They took their seats in the new and commodious car and soon reached the little house. The ingrain and rag carpets had disappeared. In their places were Oriental rugs. Striped red awnings shaded the windows and piazzas. The porch had been converted into the cosiest of lounging places with willow furniture, scarlet cushions, rugs, birds, plants, etc., as well as small tables filled with the latest magazines and Aunt Susan's sewing baskets. They had a hammock at either end, and altogether it was lovely. Mrs. Hollister simply raved over it and the artistic interior with its fine old furniture.

"Ethel is responsible for this change," said Tom, removing his hat and wiping his handsome brow. "Last summer when she came here I dressed like a countryman, but in the most tactful manner she suggested high collars, different ties, and fairly talked my army hat right off my head, saying that I looked like a G.A.R. Little by little she's converted Aunt Susan into a fashionable woman. But how careless of me. Let me get you a cup of tea," he said to Mrs. Hollister, placing a table before her and a stool under her feet.

He soon returned, bringing the tray and a plate of delicious jumbles.

"You see," he continued, "Aunt Susan will not keep two girls, so I have to be waitress now and then. She is attached to Jane, who though is a good cook, but her trouble is she's set in her way and refuses to stay if we allow another girl to enter the house. We are handicapped, you see, for we can't spare Jane, nor could we replace her."

Gradually he took Mrs. Hollister into his confidence and told her of his early life and of Aunt Susan's misfortunes. "But bless you," he continued, "the Lord is good to us. She'll never need a penny for my income is increasing and my practice is more than I can attend to. I should have a partner but she won't hear of my taking one. She is too cautious. So I have several young students who study law in my office and help me as well."

Then he proceeded to extol Ethel.

"Mrs. Hollister," he said, "she's a girl of wonderful character and she'll make a magnificent woman. I notice she's improved since she was here."

"Yes, it's her college," replied her mother, "and the life at camp last summer. I must admit she knew more than I when she broke loose from my foolish and unwise influence. I was not fit to guide her, Mr. Harper, I realize it now."

"Never mind, madam; it's to you she owes her beauty. Why, you and she look exactly like sisters," whereupon Mrs. Hollister capitulated to Tom Harper. She couldn't speak of him with enough enthusiasm and praise. She wrote pages to Archibald.

"My dear, everyone says he'll yet be Governor, and while I wouldn't have you breathe it for the world I'm sure he's in love with Ethel. What a couple they'd make. Of course she has no suspicion of such a thing, nor would I hint it to her; but you wait and see."

Mr. Hollister smiled as he read his wife's letter, and his heart was glad. He had known Tom Harper's father and had respected him highly.

"Well," he thought, "this time Bella is on the right tack. I'll not interfere," and he softly whistled "Comin' Thro' the Rye."

CHAPTER V

CAMP AGAIN

"Aunt Susan, you've grown so young," said Ethel, "and as for Tom, well he's the glass of fashion and mould of form. He looks fine. Oh! I'm so glad to be back and to have Mother and Grandmother with me; and Father will be here soon. It seems like a dream — too good to be true. Hasn't Mother grown lovely?"

"Never saw anything like the change," replied the old lady. "In fact, you've worked wonders in us all, my dear," she said. "Look at me. Why! I feel like an up-to-date fashion plate."

Ethel laughed.

"Yes, Madam, you're up-to-date all right and no mistake. I didn't know you that day at the depot."

"I often wonder," continued the elderly woman, "if people think I'm putting on airs. Really, Jane told me of some woman who said 'old Mrs. Carpenter was mighty upraised, dressing like a young girl.' It's funny, isn't it, what dress will do. But I should look young for I'm so happy to have Alice here again, and to think that we shall be together all summer. I don't yet seem to realize it."

"Did you notice how Grandmother cried as this house came to view, — her birthplace?"

"No wonder. She hasn't been here," said Aunt Susan, "since Mother's funeral, I presume it brought it all back to her. Poor Alice! I ought not to say it, but Archie Hollister was not the man to make her happy. He ran through with nearly all of her money. It slipped through his fingers just like water, and I guess her life with his family was none too peaceful and happy. They had the name of being great fighters. Of course she has her recompense in John and Archibald — that's something. A woman needs peace. Now take your mother, for instance. Why has she grown young? Because she's quit worrying — that is the secret."

"Yes, and when I think that she did it all for me — why, Aunt Susan,
I can't lay up anything against her; I love her too well. She sees
now how useless it all was. But what do you know about Harvey Bigelow?
Isn't he developing into a fine man?"

"He certainly is," replied Aunt Susan, "and I always liked him. He looked
one squarely in the eye, and such a man can be trusted."

"I don't know," answered Ethel, "of late everyone seems to be changing for
the better. The whole world appears different to me. It makes me happy to
see others happy," and the girl went out to call her mother and Tom in to
tea.

"I'm transferring my allegiance to your mother, young woman," said Tom.

"I'm not a bit jealous," replied Ethel. "Mother is really more interesting to
men than I, and what's more, she's always been. But hurry in; Jane will be
furious if her biscuits grow cold."

The two weeks passed only too quickly. They spent their days touring all
over Ohio, so it seemed to Ethel, and at night the young people came in
shoals to see her, while the grown-ups had bridge parties. Said Mrs.
Hollister:

"How hospitable and lovely these Westerners are. I had no idea that they
were so refined."

"What did you expect to meet, Mother?" laughed Ethel — "not cowboys?"

"Susan," said Grandmother one morning, "I notice that you curl your hair.
It's very becoming, I think."

"Alice, you don't consider me too old, do you? Sometimes I wonder if I'm
not sort of making a fool of myself, but Ethel got me in the way of it and I
try to keep the front as fluffy as possible, for she asked me to. And I've
another confession to make," said Aunt Susan. "Alice, I blue my hair —

regular bluing water so as to keep it white. There now — what do you think of that?"

"So do I, Susan," laughed her sister. "I've done it for several years. It certainly does improve the color. Grey hairs grow so yellow looking. The child is right. We ought to keep ourselves up while we're able. We polish up old mahogany and keep it fresh and clean — why not old women?" and the two laughed merrily.

"I think the Camp Fire business has made a woman of Ethel, don't you?"

"How could it fail to?" said Aunt Susan. "Women are coming into their own, Alice. They're growing sensible and self-reliant. Look at our Grandmothers and at us. Do you notice the difference? And our grandchildren will be just as far ahead of us as we are of our grandmothers. Isn't it wonderful?"

"I like you Western people," said Mrs. Hollister, coming in at that moment followed by Ethel.

"I've just told Mother," said the girl, "that Western people can give points to us. They are natural, kind-hearted, hospitable, and they seldom measure their friendship by the amount of people's bank accounts. With them it's character that talks."

"How did you like my sanitarium, Bella?" asked Aunt Susan.

"I couldn't half express myself," replied Mrs. Hollister. "You're a wonderful woman, Aunt Susan, and the people here have cause to bless you. I've never before admitted this to Ethel, but I'm very glad that she came here last summer. I see my short-sightedness every day when I look back and realize how I was bringing her up," and Mrs. Hollister wiped her eyes.

"You've been a lovely and kind mother to me," replied Ethel. "You have sacrificed far too much for me and I never half appreciated it."

17

"I have been an unwise mother my dear," said she, "and you stopped me just in time. I only now begin to realize my limitations. I've been self-centered and conceited."

Ethel kissed her mother affectionately, and the two old ladies coughed and knitted vigorously.

"We are all liable to make mistakes, Bella," said Aunt Susan. "Yours has been in loving your child too dearly."

CHAPTER VI

UNCLE JOHN'S

They arrived in Columbus where Uncle John greeted them affectionately and insisted upon kissing his sister-in-law. Mrs. Hollister was persuaded not to go to camp until after a few days, when the girls should be settled. Then Uncle John was to take her up. So Ethel, Kate, and the girls, with one new member, went alone.

Save that Nora Casey wore mourning and seemed quiet, everything was the same as the summer before. Patty Sands was wild with delight upon seeing Ethel. Edna Whitely was the same happy-go-lucky Edna as of old. Mollie Long and Edith Overman had grown very tall, while Sallie Davis had become a perfect roly poly. She had gained twenty pounds and was constantly dieting and taking long walks.

Mattie Hastings cried when she beheld Ethel. Mattie had grown quiet and dignified, while in her face she showed more character.

Ethel looked at them all, especially at Honora.

"Can I not put my dislike of that girl behind me?" she thought. "Why can't I be nice to her?"

She tried hard. She began asking her of her mother, and tears filled Nora's eyes, but after a while her voice began to take on its old shrill tones, while in her manner there came that indescribable something that had always repelled Ethel.

"That girl is my cross," she thought. "I must like her, and yet I can't.

I shall never become worthy to be a Camp Fire Girl until I overcome it.

I wonder if she'll affect Mother as she does me."

Ethel was now a Fire Maker. In addition to her Wood Gatherer's ring she wore the pretty silver bracelet of the Fire Maker.

The second evening they had a Council Fire. The wood and kindling had been gathered and brought by Edna Whitely and a new girl named Kate Winthrop, who had never been to Camp before. Edna couldn't seem to advance. She was actually too lazy to work for honors and it worried Kate Hollister not a little.

"What's the difference?" she would say. "Someone will have to gather wood and we have but one new girl—that's Kate. You may be glad that I stayed."

The girls looked pretty in their brown ceremonial gowns and their long hair banded with the ceremonial band. Ethel advanced and lighted the fire, intoning the usual Fire Makers' song. Then they had the exercises. Honors were awarded and several girls advanced to the next higher grade. This is the Fire Makers' ode to Fire that they intoned as Ethel lighted the Council Fire: "Oh, Fire, long years ago when our fathers fought with the great animals you were their protection. From the cruel cold of winter you saved them. When they needed food you changed the flesh of beasts into savory meat for them. During all the ages your mysterious flame has been a symbol to them for Spirit. So (tonight) we light our fire in remembrance of the great Spirit who gave you to us."

In the darkness of the woods with the bright flames shooting upward the effect of the chanting was weird, mysterious and unusual.

Then Kate showed Ethel the typed copy of the Legend of Ohio which had been attached to each count book, handing her a copy for her own.

The roll was called, reports read of the last Council Fire, and of the weekly meeting. Edna Whitely had really exerted herself and had written it in clever rhyme.

Then to their surprise a report of Ethel's and Patty's kindness to Mattie Hastings was read. It seems that Mattie's conscience had troubled her and at one of the meetings she had confessed it all and how she had been saved by the two girls. She also requested that it should be read upon Ethel's return. It told how under unusual distress she had been tempted to do a great wrong,—-how the two girls caused her to make restitution, and how after that they placed Mollie in the Cripples School, and that now she was on her way to recovery. It said that she began from then to try and lead a better life and that with God's help she was doing so.

The girls looked at one another, but although they made no sign they knew what the wrong was. But they smiled at Mattie in the most friendly way, Nora grasping her by the hand said:

"I hope yere sister will be after walkin' soon."

Then came the Wohelo ceremony. Mattie came forward and lighted a branch, throwing it on the ashes, while Patty Sands knelt and lighted it chanting:

"Wohelo means work. We glorify work because through work we are free. We work to win, to conquer, to be masters. We work for the joy of working and because we are free."

Then she stepped back and Edith Overman came forward chanting and lighting another branch.

"Wohelo means health. We hold on to health because through health we serve and are happy; in caring for the health and beauty of our persons we are caring for the very shrine of the Great Spirit. Wohelo means health."

Then Sallie Davis stepped forward while Edith retired. She lighted the third branch which crackled and threw up numberless red sparks, after which she chanted the last verse:

"I light the light of love, for Wohelo means love. We love Love, for love is life and light and joy and sweetness. And love is comradeship and motherhood and fatherhood, and all dear kinship. Love is the joy of service so deep that self is forgotten. Wohelo means love."

After that this song was sung:

"Lay me to sleep in thy sheltering flame.

    O Master of the Hidden Fire.

Wash pure my heart and cleanse for me
    My Soul's desire.
In flame of sunrise bathe my soul
    O Master of the Hidden Fire.
That when I wake clear-eyed may be
    My Soul's desire."
This is by Fiona Macleod.

They stood around talking to Miss Kate for a little while, who walking over to Mattie kissed her tenderly, after which each girl followed her example before retiring, and poor Mattie was all broken up over it.

CHAPTER VII

MRS. HOLLISTER'S VISIT TO CAMP

When the morning dawned on the day Mrs. Hollister was expected, great were the preparations made for that lady.

"Listen to me, girls; she's the cleverest woman you ever met," said Cousin Kate. "She has not been exactly in favor of our organization, so I wish each of you girls to do your best, and Mrs. Hollister can teach you so many useful things."

"Yes, indeed," said Ethel. "Cousin Kate is right. There's very little that Mother can not do."

Old Mr. Adams came up with a load of delicacies which had been ordered by the thoughtful Uncle John.

He paid no attention to the girls but as on previous occasions he gave his entire attention to his horses. He wiped off their foaming sweat with his hands. Last year it had been his handkerchief varied with bundles of grass and leaves. After cleaning them to his satisfaction he calmly walked to the clear brook and washed his hands thoroughly.

"Isn't that awful?" whispered Patty to Miss Kate. "I shall never feel like drinking water from that brook again."

"Why my dear," laughed Kate, "that water changes every minute. It's gone now and in its place there's fresh — don't worry."

"Here they are!" called Nora, and there came to view Uncle John and a lady whom from Ethel's resemblance to her they at once knew and fell deeply in love with, especially Mattie.

And everything pleased Mrs. Hollister, — the girls, their costumes, their tents, and the delicious dinner cooked over an open fire interested her greatly. She even held one of the forked branches on which reposed the chicken and broiled it as well as a chef, but she thought the green corn was the most delicious thing that she'd ever tasted. After dinner she said:

"Now girls, see if I have it correct: 'After tying a string to the end of each ear, soak the corn in water for an hour. Then lay it on the hot coals, turning frequently. Draw it out by the string and eat with salt and melted butter.' Well, it's simply great. I wish I were young again. I think I'd like to be a Camp Fire Girl." She was as enthusiastic as a child. Ethel looked at Kate and they smiled over the change that had taken place since the day Kate wished to explain to her aunt what the Camp Fire Girl was.

"Don't you think that Mother grows young?" asked Ethel proudly of her cousin.

"She's a changed woman," replied Kate, "in every way. She's simply lovely."

Mrs. Hollister adapted herself and made friends quickly. She became tactful, a quality that had hitherto been unknown. She liked Nora and the girl loved Mrs. Hollister. Ethel marveled. That her mother who disliked anything savoring of loudness could tolerate Nora seemed wonderful.

"The fault must lie with me," she thought. "Even Mother likes her."

Mrs. Hollister went right to work and taught the girls how to cut and fit. She taught them many of the little arts and niceties of dressmaking, and the girls became proficient and at the next Council meeting each received several honors. Then she taught them to trim hats and make the daintiest bows; and after she had taught them how to crochet and make Irish lace their gratitude was boundless.

She also taught them how to cook—how to make delicious corn bread with one egg, where they had been in the habit of using two, insisting upon their first scalding their meal. Then she made them delicious gingerbread, using cold coffee left from breakfast in place of milk or cream and many other dishes of which they had never heard.

"Really, Aunt Bella," said Kate, as the girls were receiving their honors, "I feel that you deserve some of these beads."

CHAPTER VIII
THE SCOUTS ARRIVE

Great was the surprise of the girls when the next afternoon they beheld walking towards the Camp two young men in Scout costume. They were none other than Harvey Bigelow and young Teddy Kip, the Master and assistant Scout Master of the "Flying Eagles" Scout Patrol. Each wore a small flag, and upon a red ground was a black and white eagle. As they advanced they gave their cry — "Yeh — yeh — yeh!"

"Oh! Harvey," screamed Ethel, and rushed forward, greeting them warmly.

Then Cousin Kate came and welcomed them cordially, introducing them to the nine girls.

"Why, Mrs. Hollister," said Harvey, catching sight of her in her tent, "it does seem good to see you here," and he gazed at her thoughtfully and curiously. "'Pon my word you've grown so young I thought you were Ethel at first."

She wore one of her daughter's costumes and really she did look wonderfully youthful.

"Well, you can't complain. The Camp life has done you some good, and there you were so down on it."

"Yes, I was, but people change. Look at yourself," replied she seriously.

"Mrs. Hollister," said he, "I've been here only one week, but I already feel that I'm another man. It's splendid for both boy and girl. It's a boon to be able to get away from city people and fashionable resorts. Nan has put up a big fight and, Ethel, she's coming out to see you next month," he said.

"Oh, how lovely! Kate, hear this: Nannie Bigelow is coming here to see us next month."

"I shall be here until the middle," said Harvey, "and she'll go home with us. I've an aunt in Springfield and she'll go there for a visit first. After that she'll come on here and spend a few days if you girls want her to."

25

"I'm so glad," said Ethel, and she ran to tell her mother.

Teddy Kip was a handsome lad of about eighteen. Immediately Patty Sands suggested that he must see everything, so she took him off under her wing. The rest sat on the ground while Harvey related several anecdotes and funny experiences that had befallen his patrol since they came to Camp.

"Now you must stay and dine with us," said Kate. "Our cooking may not surprise you, as it is the Scouts' way as well, but we'll give you a change — a shore dinner. Father sent up some very fresh clams. We'll steam them, and we'll have roasted potatoes, corn, and broiled chicken, a little salad and a ripe watermelon to finish."

"Well, I declare — 'pon my word, one might imagine himself in Rhode

Island. We'll stay," and he smacked his lips.

"Nora, will you take Mr. Bigelow and show him our cellar. And the boys — perhaps they'll help us to prepare our meal," said Kate.

The young fellows were delighted to help the girls. Nora arose slowly and

Harvey followed.

Kate remarked to Ethel that Nora had changed so since her mother's death and asked her if she had noticed it.

"Yes, I do notice that she seems more quiet," replied Ethel.

"But you still dislike her though?" asked Kate.

"I don't know," replied Ethel. "I'm ashamed to admit it, Cousin Kate, but I can never seem to overcome that antipathy to her. If only her voice would lower a little, and if she'd cease to come up and slap one on the back I might feel differently, but she's so rough and unladylike."

"Ethel, environments may have had much to do with that. She seems to love your mother. But here comes Patty with young Kip."

"What a dandy site you have here for a Camp," said the young man. "Gee! it's choice. It beats ours."

When dinner was ready how they ate! They pronounced it equal to the best shore dinner ever prepared, and when finished there was nothing left excepting clam shells and corn cobs.

That was Mrs. Hollister's last day in Camp. She had been with the girls for two weeks. After leaving Camp she was to spend half of her time with Kate's parents and the remaining with Aunt Susan.

Harvey and Teddy stayed until nearly five o'clock, and it was with regret on both sides that they had to go.

The next day being Sunday, Kate read the prayers while they all sung several hymns, after which each girl was left to do as she chose. Ethel proposed to ride horseback. Several joined together and hired a buckboard for the afternoon.

"We'll meet you at the Lake," they said to Ethel, and off they went.

It was a warm afternoon. The sky looked alternately bright, then cloudy, but they started not minding though it rained.

Nora declined to join the buckboard party and strolled off by herself. She looked almost pretty in her clean, white linen suit and her hair tightly bound by a broad black ribbon. The goldenrod and sumac were opening, but the summer flowers looked old and tired, as though they needed new gowns and freshening up a bit. The girl thought of how alone she was and sighed. Then her mother came into her mind. To think that she had to be taken while so young—not yet forty-five, and the tears rolled down her cheeks. But "Thank God," she thought, "I never caused her any unhappiness, and I still have my dear, kind father," and Nora wiped her eyes. "It's Miss Ethel who dislikes me. No matter what I say to her nor how friendly I am, she won't like me. And when I try to joke or do her a little kindness, if she smiles sure her smile chills me. It's like a piece of ice going down me back. And her 'thank you, Honora' is as cold as charity. I like her mother the best. And yet Miss Ethel kissed me goodbye at the train last summer; but she was kissing everyone and I suppose she had to kiss me, for she's too much of a lady to slight a body. Yet she'd be glad to see the last of me—that I know."

CHAPTER IX

NORA GIVES SERVICE

Honora was an unconscious lover of Nature. She turned and beheld the sun slowly sinking.

"Ah! it must be nearly six o'clock," she thought. "I must make haste," but she stood spellbound, watching the glowing crimson, purple and yellow changing into orange, green, and greyish pink, and she gazed at the fiery ball sinking slowly behind the hills.

"How lovely!" she thought, "and it's gone down in a cloud. That means rain. It's growing very dark. Me for a quick walk down these hills before I lose my way."

She started down the path not a little worried. She had strayed off the main road and was on a side one leading through the woods. If only it would keep light until she reached Camp, and then if she could strike the broad road she'd be all right.

Walking rapidly through the woods she suddenly fancied that she hard a low moan, as though from someone in pain.

"It's a tramp perhaps," she thought. "He may be in trouble. Well, tramp or no tramp I must help him. I'll see."

Unafraid, Nora walked to the spot whence the cry had proceeded. Her eye fell upon an object huddled together on the ground. As it was out of the beaten path she stepped from branches and logs to stones and rocks before she reached it. She stooped down and gazed at it intently; then she uttered an exclamation of surprise.

"It's Miss Ethel!" she gasped. "God help her."

She was right. There lay Ethel Hollister—the girl who had never liked her—the girl from whom, no matter how hard she might try, Nora could get nothing beyond a cool "Thank you very much, Nora."

From the arm of this young woman trickled a stream of bright, red blood.

29

Honora wondered if she was dead. She gently shook her.

"Miss Ethel!" she called once and twice, "Are ye much hurt?" Then she half lifted her to a sitting posture and Ethel opened her eyes.

"Oh, Miss Casey—Honora!" she gasped feebly. "Thank God it is you who have found me. I have been so frightened. Two men were searching for me. I passed them on the road before my horse took fright and threw me. I heard them say: 'It must be the same girl. She rode a white horse. Now I know who she is. She's the niece of John Hollister. Her father is a rich New Yorker. We can sell the horse. We've got him safe, and we can keep the girl for a ransom. Probably she's injured and is lying somewhere around here.' Nora, I dared not breathe lest they should find me. I prayed to God as I've never prayed before to let them pass me and to send me help. He has answered my prayer and I'm grateful. When I heard your footsteps I thought they had returned. Oh! I am so glad that it's you," and she burst into tears.

Nora knelt down and took her by the hand.

"Where is your pain, my dear?" she asked.

"My leg. I guess it must be broken, and my arm—-I have had that nearly cut off. The horse became frightened and unmangeable. He turned into these woods and started to run. I was knocked off by the branch of a tree. I don't know how long I've lain here—it seems for hours. I must have fainted, but Nora the pain in my arm and leg is terrible. Whatever can we do?"

The girl's hat hung from the tree. Her hair was unloosed and hanging about her face. Evidently she was suffering agony, and to make matters worse upon the leaves overhead Nora heard a pattering of rain.

"This will never do," she said to herself. Not a sign of a house or a vehicle in sight. A damp chill pervaded the air. They were too far from the main road to seek assistance.

"Your arm has been cut by this jagged stone, Miss Ethel," said Nora, kneeling and starting to roll from the girl's arm the sleeve of her blouse. "I don't think there are any bones broken. But first I must stop its bleeding."

Nora, having had considerable experience with cuts, wounds and bruises, went to work as though she were about to teach the girls "first aid."

Her handkerchief was soiled. Ethel had lost hers. Both women wore silk petticoats. How could she manage to secure a bandage?

Suddenly her mother wit came to the rescue. She slipped off her linen skirt. It was perfectly clean. With her strong teeth she tore into strips the front breadth.

"Hark!" she exclaimed. "Glory be to God! I think I hear running water." She said it devoutly and in gratitude, for now it was water that she needed. Taking Ethel's hat from the tree she started up the road where to her joy she beheld a watering trough that was fed by a little waterfall trickling down the side of the rocks.

After thoroughly washing the long linen strips so as to be sure that the starch was out of them she filled Ethel's hat with water and hurried back.

"Here, dearie," she said, "Let me wash your face. I brought the water in your hat," and with the balance of her skirt she washed the girl's face and then proceeded to tear open the sleeve, cleansing the wound with a fresh hatful of water. She did it carefully and thoroughly, with the skill of a surgeon. It was an ugly wound, but she bound the arm firmly with the strips.

"There now! So much for that," ejaculated Nora, rising and pushing back from her brow one curly lock that always insisted upon falling over her eyes.

"Oh, Honora! you are an angel," exclaimed Ethel, "and I have always been so unfriendly."

Nora appeared not to hear but went on:

31

"Can you stand, my dear?" she asked.

"No," sobbed the girl, "I guess my leg must be broken. However are we to reach Camp? Oh, Nora, for God's sake don't leave me. I should die of fright were you to do so, and the men may be hiding near even now. Don't go, I beseech. I know I am selfish and I've been unkind to you, but forgive me, Nora. I'll be your slave after this if only you'll stay with me. Don't go for help. Just stay here until I die," and the girl fell to sobbing.

"I'm cold," she murmured — "I'm so chilly, Nora," and she shivered.

Quickly Nora removed her heavy white sweater that she had just put on, and raising Ethel to a sitting posture she first put in her good arm. Then she fastened the sweater about the girl's neck.

"There, dear, that will keep you warm, and I'll not be after leaving you — never fear — not if we stay together all night in these woods. But I must think how we can manage with you and your injuries. Faith it's raining and you may catch your death."

"And I have your sweater on, Nora!" exclaimed Ethel. "Oh, how selfish I am."

"Keep still," replied Nora. "I couldn't wear it now, for I'm going to try and carry you home."

For a moment Nora gazed tentatively at Ethel. Then suddenly there appeared a dawn of hope in her strong honest face.

"Miss Ethel, listen," she began. "When a child did ye ever play pig-a-back? Perhaps I might get you home that way."

"Yes, Nora. Papa always carried me up to bed that way," and the girl burst into tears.

"Ye mustn't cry," said Nora. "If ye do I shan't be able to carry ye. Now wipe your pretty eyes and help me carry ye as Papa used to. Forget your pain and try to be patient, for, Ethel, we must reach camp some way. Doubtless they are searching for us even now, but this is a side road far from the main one. They'll never think to look here, nor could they hear us were we of call. And then those men you spoke of. They may be near. There's no time to lose. Get on my back and cling for dear life."

Nora had great sense. She realized that until she had thoroughly frightened Ethel she would not exert herself and forget her pain. Then, too, if what she had told her were true, the men might really be lying in wait to capture the supposed wealthy New York girl.

Sitting on the ground with her back before Ethel she first gently raised the wounded arm, bringing the other one around to meet it. Thanks to the low branch of a tree and to Nora's recent physical culture exercises, making an almost superhuman effort she arose with her burden on her back. Then grasping the girl's knees she held them firmly, thereby supporting her injured leg, and started for the road, stopping now and then by a fence or stone to take breath and rest. On and on in that failing light she bravely walked.

As she descended the hill she seemed to have gained new strength. Now and then she'd speak cheering words to the wounded girl, trying to encourage her to bear her pain. The rain pelted in Honora's face, often blinding her. The thunder rolled and the lightning played, but she showed no sign of faltering. Onward she went, even faster.

Soon to her joy she beheld the main road, and after a few more rods a light from the Camp Fire.

"Shure," she thought, "now I know why men in olden times looked for the fire from their camps. It does cheer a body and give them new life."

She was ready to drop when she reached Camp. Ethel was no light weight. While in Camp she had gained, and now she weighed nearly a hundred and thirty-seven pounds. As Nora neared home she saw parties of men about to start on searching tours. They had sent word by Mr. Adams to Harvey, and there he and his patrol stood ready to start. Uncle John with the second party were there as well. In some way the horse had escaped from the two men and had returned to Camp, but without Ethel. Then they knew that she had been thrown. And as for Nora, something dreadful must have happened to her, for Nora was so strong and self-reliant.

A shout rent the air when they beheld Nora Casey drenched to the skin, hatless, coatless, with nearly all of her skirt missing, and carrying on her back a hysterical, shrieking girl, while with no apparent effort she walked steadily towards them. Harvery Bigelow's admiration for one so strong and courageous showed itself on every line of his face.

Uncle John took Ethel from Nora and laid her on the Camp bed that had been brought from the tent.

"By Jove!" ejaculated Harvey as he examined Ethel's ankle and pronounced it a compound fracture, "you're all right, Miss Casey, first to staunch the blood and bandage her arm, and second to bind her ankle in such a surgeon-like manner, say nothing of carrying her on your back for over a mile and a half and holding her leg so that you saved her pain. I take off my hat to you, Miss Casey. You have the nerve and strength of a man."

"I don't see," said Uncle John, "how in the name of heaven you managed to raise her, wounded as she was, upon your back—let alone bringing her through the pouring rain a dark night like this. Why! it's been a regular thunder shower. I'm glad that her mother knows nothing of it."

Nora sighed. She was very tired. Miss Kate came forward and put her arm around her.

"My dear, you are an honor to the Camp Fires. We owe a vote of thanks to this brave girl," and taking Nora's face between her hands she kissed her affectionately.

"I've done nothing wonderful," replied Nora simply, taking her sweater from Patty Sands. "Luckily I heard her moan and found her. I couldn't go away and leave her helpless and alone in a blinding storm, and two men waiting to seize her." Then she told Ethel's story of the conversation that she had overheard.

"Nor could we stay in the woods over night alone."

A buckboard appeared and Mrs. Hollister jumped out. She had heard of the accident through Mr. Adams and had made him bring her up.

After seeing Ethel for a few moments she rushed out and threw her arms about Nora.

"You are a dear brave girl," she sobbed, kissing her. "You have saved

Ethel's life. Never while I live shall I forget it."

"Nor I," broke in Uncle John, grasping the hands of the girl. "Miss Nora, you're a fine young woman and you're father has cause to be proud of his daughter."

"Miss Nora," ejaculated Harvey, "allow me to congratulate you. You're a dead game sport," and he wrung her hands heartily, after which Teddy Kip grasped her by the arm saying:

"Why, Miss Casey, you're a regular Scout—you are, and no mistake."

Nora smiled faintly.

"Thank you all," she said. "I am very tired. I think I shall go to bed.

Good night."

CHAPTER X

A HEROINE

So Nora Casey became the heroine of the Camp. An account of her bravery was in all the papers and the entire Camp was written up. The once neglected and disliked girl was now in a fair way to be spoiled. But Nora could not be spoiled. She was too sensible.

"I say, Miss Nora," exclaimed Harvey the next day, "I don't think I'd dare marry a woman with your strength. You'd put me to shame."

Nora laughed good naturedly.

"Quit yere blarney," she said.

As for Ethel, she couldn't bear to let Nora out of her sight, and Nora whose heart was tender and whose nature was forgiving devoted herself to the girl, reading aloud, relating funny stories of her father, and when tired of talking Patty, Mattie, she and Ethel would play bridge.

The men considered that Ethel had had a narrow escape. Uncle John consulted with Judge Sands as to what was best to do about the kidnapers. A few days later two suspicious looking creatures were arrested. They had escaped from Joliet jail and admitted having been for days in the woods. Ethel rode to the trial and identified their voices but she had not seen their faces. They were returned to jail in Joliet and before they left they confessed that they had contemplated finding the girl and holding her for a ransom. They were intending to sell the horse but they had not tied him securely and he had broken loose. They were ugly looking customers.

The next week before the breaking up of camp, when Mr. Casey came to take Nora home, everyone flocked around him telling of his daughter's brave act. He took Ethel by the hand and remarked simply:

"It was like Honora to do that. There's none more brave than she—God bless her."

From that day Nora had no better friend than Ethel. She felt that the girl had saved her life and her gratitude was boundless.

"Tell me," asked; Nora, "why did you dislike me so?"

"I was wicked, Nora," replied Ethel, "I am ashamed of it now."

"But," persisted the girl, "did you think me vulgar?"

"No," replied Ethel. "I thought you had a loud voice, and there's something about a loud voice that I dislike. But even so I should have overlooked that, had I been a good girl. You are so far above me, Nora, that I am ashamed to even acknowledge it."

"Miss Ethel—" said Nora.

"Call me Ethel in future," said the girl—"please do."

"Well—Ethel—you are not the first one who has criticised my voice. My teachers have always done so, and even my mother used to say, 'Not so loud, Nora dear. Speak more gentle like.'"

"Did she?" asked Ethel.

"Yes, my mother had her faults, Ethel, but at heart she was a lady. So your dislike of me was not so strange after all."

"But," interrupted Ethel, "Nora, perhaps I wasn't thankful to hear your loud voice when I lay there wounded and helpless, and I'm ashamed to even have told you."

"I wish you to help me," broke in Nora. "I wish to make myself different— more of a lady. Will you tell me when I talk too loud? It will be a favor if you will."

Ethel assented and kissed Nora affectionately.

Nannie Bigelow arrived and the girl became a general favorite. She at once fell in love with Nora.

"Why, she's a heroine," she said. "She'd give her life for another. I think she's splendid."

Nannie had much to say of their New York Camp Fire, and of the girls who belonged.

"You know some of them are quite unlike us, but Miss Westcott says they'll improve—that being with us will make them more gentle. And you have no idea how they are improving. And as for Dorothy's nursery, it's just booming. There is a waiting list a mile long," and she chatted on, entertaining the girls with her talk.

At the next and last Council Meeting, the girls received honors for having slept three months out of doors, for learning to swim, and rowing twenty miles on the Muskingum River, and for sailing a boat without help for fifty miles. They also received extra honors for cooking, and for learning and making a mattress out of the twigs of trees; for long walks, and for washing and ironing, which the girls did well.

Whenever she looked at Nora, Ethel's conscience troubled her. She seemed to feel her own unworthiness. Mrs. Hollister suggested to Mr. Casey that Nora should visit them for a couple of months in the city.

"I'll gladly let her go to ye next winter, Ma'am, but not to visit. I would like her to be wid a grand lady like yourself, and if you'll let me pay her board I'll consider it a great favor. And if she might go to some fine school, Ma'am, where she could learn how to be a lady and stay at your house I would pay any price."

At first Mrs. Hollister objected to the money part, but Mr. Casey begged so hard that, realizing what Nora had done for Ethel, she felt she should be willing to do anything to benefit her. So she consented.

"You can put me anywhere," said Nora, "I will be like one of your family."

Mrs. Hollister put her arm around the girl.

"My dear," she said, "the best I have ought not to be good enough for you. It's little enough for me to take you, and I should like to do so without having your father pay me a penny."

So it was all arranged. In November, Nora was to become an inmate of the Hollister household.

Ethel had made up her mind to give the girl her room, she taking one on the top floor.

"I would gladly sleep on bare boards for her," she said to her mother, — "the brave girl to whom I have been so unjust. I'm glad she's coming. I'll devote all my extra time to her happiness."

CHAPTER XI

BREAKING UP OF CAMP AND A SURPRISE

The time had arrived for the girls to separate. The Scouts came up and carried Nannie off. She had become a great favorite. As Patty expressed it, Nannie was a comfortable visitor because she seemed to "belong." She made no fuss and adapted herself to their ways.

She promised to return the following summer and Harvey pronounced their camp as fine as any place they might select.

"So there's no reason why we boys should not come back, too; but you must let us entertain you Camp Fire girls next year. It's been all on your side this."

So they all went to the train to see them off, and people crowded around as though they might be a circus troupe, staring curiously at them and making remarks.

Then after saying goodbye the different members went to their homes.

Ethel and her cousin Kate were to go to Akron for a week or so, as

Uncle Archie Hollister was coming up to spend his vacation.

The girls met him at the train and Ethel was overjoyed.

"Oh, Papa," she said, "if only you could have been here before Camp broke up. But we are going up for the day and give you a regular Camp Fire dinner," and she kissed him affectionately.

"Next year I'll get off earlier," replied Mr. Hollister, "but our

President was very ill and none of us liked to leave."

They gave Mr. Hollister a rousing dinner. Nearly all of the girls were present. They did their cooking like desserts, bread, etc., at home, but the meat, corn and potatoes were roasted on the coals. They had Uncle John, Judge Sands, Mr. Casey and Mr. Hollister for guests, and everything went off finely. Mr. Hollister was loud in his praises of the cooking, and in fact, the whole organization.

"It's great," he said, smacking his lips. "I think the person who invented it should have a gold medal."

They spent a few days at Columbus. Ethel went to see Mattie and her mother. She also spent the night with Nora. Their home was very handsome and Ethel could not help but respect kind-hearted Mr. Casey, who tried to make it so pleasant for her. She had grown very fond of Nora. She saw her good traits,—her splendid unselfishness, and her tenderness towards her father as she tried to take her mother's place with him.

"What a narrow, selfish girl I've been," she thought, "never to have noticed them before. Why, the way Nora shielded Mattie when the girl took her ring was a lesson to me, and I never took it."

During their stay at Uncle John's Mrs. Hollister came up, and the meeting between her husband and self was like lovers. Ethel was glad.

"And it was I that kept them apart," she told Kate—"I with my society and expensive schools. Poor Father! what could he do but grind from morning until night; and Mother with her hopes and ambitions—what could she do? Why, they had no time to speak to each other except on business and money. It was all so false and wrong. Now they are as they should have been, but think of the lost years, and all for me." "Never think of it, Ethel," said Kate, "it's past and over. Everything has come smooth. Forget it, dear; you were not to blame."

Judge Sands called nearly every evening. He and Uncle Archie struck up quite a friendship. The Judge took him on auto trips far into the country, Kate, Patty, and Ethel going along.

One evening, after they all had gone back to Akron, Judge Sands called

Patty into the library.

"I wish to have a little talk with you, my dear," he said.

41

"Are you going to scold me for running over my allowance last month?" she replied, "because if you are I just couldn't help it. I wanted to give all of the girls a little remembrance, and — "

"Patty, my child, have I ever scolded you for anything — think? Haven't you done exactly as you chose since your childhood?"

"Yes," replied the girl, "but I know that there are times when you should scold me, Papa, for I know I am self-willed and disobedient."

"Well, we shall forget that. You're a pretty good girl considering that you have but one parent. Now this is what I wish to see you about. Your mother died when you were three, dear, and you've been with me ever since. It's been lonely for both of us at times, and for me especially so while you are away at school. Patty, how should you like a mother? Of course, no one can take the place of her who has gone, but I mean another one."

The girl began to cry.

"I should not like it, Papa."

Then she looked at him. He was a handsome man, and if ever she were to marry he would be alone, in the prime of life.

"I suppose I'm selfish," she sobbed, clinging to him, "but I should hate a stepmother. Think of her taking Mamma's place. Oh, Papa! I couldn't bear it."

"But supposing she was a woman of whom you were fond. Would you feel that way then?"

"I couldn't be fond of her."

"You might be fond of her already," said the Judge.

"Who — who can it be?" asked Patty, wiping her eyes and pushing back her hair.

The Judge smiled.

"Think, my dear."

"Is it Miss Kate Hollister?" cried the girl joyfully. "Tell me quick."

Then Judge Sands blushed like a schoolboy.

"Yes," he said, "she is the only woman who can take your mother's place, Patty. No—not that—no one can take her dear place; but she is the only woman upon earth whom I should ask to be my wife."

Then Patty jumped up and kissed her father many times.

"Oh, Papa!" she said, "why didn't you tell me at first and not frighten me to death. Oh! I should love her so, and I should never be jealous of her. Are you engaged?"

"No," laughed the Judge, "I have never asked her. I thought you deserved the compliment of being first consulted on the matter."

"But, Papa, perhaps she'll refuse you."

"That's my end of it," laughed her father, "but when I do ask her I wish to say that you desire it, too, for Kate might not think it agreeable to you."

"Papa, she's got to say 'yes.' I'll go along and make her if you wish. I'd just love her for a mother," and the girl clung to his neck and wept. "I only now realize how lonely you must have been all these years, and you've done it for me. But don't let her refuse. Tell her I desire it above all things."

"All right, dearie," said the Judge. "I'll go tonight."

"And wake me up, Papa. I shall be so anxious."

Judge Sands laughed and promised.

That night no matter how hard Patty tried she couldn't keep awake. Now that she knew who it was that her father desired she was happy, and one can always sleep when one is happy.

The Judge ran up the stairs two steps at a time and woke his daughter with a kiss.

"Will she, Papa?"

"Yes, dear," he answered. "She has been good enough to say 'yes.' We'll make her happy, won't we, Patty?"

"We shall," replied the girl. "And how young you seem to have grown!" she gasped. "I never noticed it before. I'm glad for you and I'm glad for her. She's a dear. I've always loved her and she's such a stunning looking woman, too. I tell you, we'll be proud of her, Papa."

They talked for half an hour over the virtues of Miss Kate, and each went to sleep thinking of how lovely she was.

When Kate and Patty met they said not a word, but from the quiet, sincere embrace each knew that the other would try and make her happy.

Congratulations poured in from all sides. Archie and his wife with Aunt Susan, Grandmother and Tom, motored all the way over to Columbus to offer theirs. Ethel was wild with joy.

"Why," she exclaimed, "everything is getting better! People are doing such sensible things lately, just as they should do. Isn't it wonderful? But, Tom, I always thought that you cared for Cousin Kate."

"So I have all along, but just as I was considering, in walked the Judge and took her off under my very nose. While I was a poor lawyer I felt that she might refuse me and I took no chances, but I never imagined she'd look at a man of his age. She's certainly met the one for her. What a splendid couple they'll make."

"You always were slow, Tom; that's your fault," laughed Ethel, "and you'll always get left. It serves you right."

"Yes, that's going to be my fate, I fear. Before I can muster up courage to propose, these girls will be snatched up — every one of them."

Judge Sands and Kate were to be married in November. They were to go to New York, Washington, etc., on a wedding trip, after which they were to meet Patty and sail for Egypt to be gone indefinitely.

"Oh, dear! who can take your place at Camp?" said the girls. "We'll never find another Guardian like you."

"I'll ask Louise Morehouse," said Miss Kate. "She's lovely, and very much interested in this Camp Fire movement. She'll be one of you just as I have been."

"Yes, and then she'll meet someone and go off and marry," said Mollie Long. "There should be a law against it. A Guardian should be obliged to serve for five years unmarried — it isn't fair," and the girls voted that Mollie was correct.

CHAPTER XII

MATTIE MAKES GOOD

After Camp had broken up, Mattie Hastings, who was now associated with a Woman's Exchange in Columbus, started one afternoon to call for Patty Sands. It was Saturday and the Exchange closed early. Mattie was doing well. She received a good salary and her heart was light. Her sister was beginning to walk. The doctors considered that next year she could discard her brace. The child was not only attending school but she was learning many useful things and Mattie was happy. Her mother had entirely given up the drug habit; her father was with Judge Sands and everything seemed as though it had come straight like a fairy story.

This lovely autumn afternoon they were going to Sallie Davis's to look at a wonderful centerpiece done by her mother. Mattie, whose fingers were extremely clever, had offered to do the work of copying it, while Patty was to pay for the silks, linen, etc. Then, jointly, they were to give it to Miss Kate for an engagement present. In case the servant should be out Sallie had given Patty her latch key.

"This is Sophronia's day out, and mother is going to a bridge party. I have an engagement, so here's the key. When you leave the flat, put it on the hall stand. Sophronia and mother will be back before I am, and they will let me in. I'll leave the centerpiece on the piano."

The apartment was on the seventh story and commanded a wonderful view of the city. After looking at the centerpiece and studying the different stitches the girls went to a window and looked out.

"Have you put the key on the hall stand?" asked Mattie.

"Yes," replied Patty. "I put it there when I first came in."

Suddenly Mattie exclaimed:

"I smell smoke."

They looked around. The odor was plainly perceptible.

"Let's go into the kitchen," said Patty.

Together they ran through the pantry and opened the kitchen door. The smoke was very thick.

"Why, Mattie, the house is afire!" said Patty Sands. "Let's get out quickly."

They opened the hall door, closing it tightly after them. They had far better have stayed in the apartment and have descended by the fire escape, but they thought of it too late. The hall door had locked behind them. The outer halls were black with smoke. People were rushing wildly up and down. The entrance leading to the roof was locked. The elevator boy called "last trip," and opened the iron doors. Frightened women and little children crowded in with servants and elderly people.

"Room for one more," yelled the boy, "quick, for God's sake!"

"You go, Mattie," said Patty.

"You go." Then Mattie Hastings lifted Patty Sands up bodily and fairly threw her into the crowded elevator.

"If the cable holds I'll come back, Miss," cried the boy half choked with smoke.

Through the smoke Mattie peered at the cable. Through the shaft she saw the angry flames shooting upward. The sparks were flying. The elevator had made its last trip and she realized it. She turned to the hall window and looked down upon the crowd. A ladder was raised. Someone had seen her.

"Thank God!" she said, "I may yet be saved."

The smoke was now black and the flames came nearer and nearer to the brave girl, who so unselfishly had given her place to her friend. She leaned out of the window. She watched the fireman ascending. Then she knew no more but fell back into the flames unconscious.

"I've got her," said the fireman, "but I guess she's gone. No one could live in the smoke up there. She's badly burned, too, poor girl—her back and arms. Lift her carefully, boys."

Patty rushed forward. "She has given her life for me," she shrieked. "Mattie, Mattie dear! don't you hear me? Speak—oh! speak to Patty."

The dying girl opened her eyes and half smiled. Patty knelt beside her and put her ear close to Mattie's mouth.

"Patty," she whispered, "tell Ethel that I made good."

Then she closed them wearily and the brave soul of Mattie Hastings passed on.

It took Patty Sands many years to recover from the shock of her friend's death. She was too ill to even know when the funeral took place. She had told her father and Kate of Mattie's last words. Ethel Hollister sent a telegram requesting that Mattie's funeral might be postponed until she arrived. The Camp Fire girls were the pallbearers.

Fortunately the cruel flames had left Mattie's face untouched and she looked lovely. The church was crowded to overflowing, as well as the street. The text of the sermon was:

"Greater love hath no man than he who lays down his life for a friend."

Mattie had "given service" as well as laying down her life for a friend, and the whole town marvelled at her bravery.

CHAPTER XIII

JUDGE SANDS AND KATE MARRY

In November Kate was married. The wedding was quiet, as Patty was still an invalid. They took her with them and left her at Mrs. Hollister's while they went on their trip. Nora had arrived for the winter two weeks before. Mrs. Hollister had entered her in Madam La Rue's school. Ethel had insisted upon giving Nora her room and had moved up stairs.

The three girls were sad. They talked of Mattie and Patty cried constantly. So after a while they avoided speaking of her in her presence.

Nora looked like one to the manner born. Mrs. Hollister, having carte blanche to buy for her anything she saw fit, purchased the loveliest second mourning costumes imaginable, and Nora wore them remarkably well. She had grown more quiet since Mattie's death. A great change seemed to have come over her. She was one of Madam's brightest pupils and very popular. Mrs. Hollister was genuinely fond of her and they went everywhere together.

When Mr. Casey came to New York he was surprised at the change. He'd say to Mrs. Hollister:

"Faith, ma'am, it's a perfect lady you're afther makin' of my girl. Her mother would bless you were she here," and Mrs. Hollister would reply:

"She is naturally a perfect lady, Mr. Casey, so it's not hard work. I consider Nora a very superior girl and I'm very fond of her," at which the father's eyes would grow half tearful, and he'd seem proud to hear it.

Nannie Bigelow and Nora became very intimate and she was made much of by Dorothy Kip and Sara Judson. Nora took an active interest in the Day Nursery and donated generously for its maintenance. Twice a week she'd go and read to the elder children and get on the floor and play with the younger ones, for she adored babies. She was especially sweet and generous to Grandmother, spending hours with her lest she should become

49

lonely. It was like a mother and daughter, instead of a girl and chaperon, to see Mrs. Hollister and Nora go about together.

"I wish I had a son, Nora," said that lady one day. "Then I should never have to see you leave me."

Nora blushed rosy red, saying:

"I wish you had, Mrs. Hollister. I dislike to think of our separation."

Mr. Casey sent the most wonderful barrels of apples and potatoes from his own place to the Hollisters, and when he came to New York he'd order fruit from the most expensive fruiterers to be sent three times a week, say nothing of boxes of flowers which came regularly throughout the entire winter.

CHAPTER XIV

A BIRTHDAY PRESENT

On one of Mr. Casey's flying trips to the city it happened to be Mrs. Hollister's birthday. Nora told him of the fact and after school together they whisked away in a taxi to shop. Upon their return he presented Mrs. Hollister with a large box, and in the most delicate manner begged her to accept it as a slight token of his gratitude for her interest in and kindness to Nora.

"Ye've been a mother to my girl and she loves ye well. Her own mother — God rest her soul — as I've often told ye, would be proud of her, and she'd know better what to give a lady, but if ye'll accept these, ma'am, Nora and I will be pleased."

Mrs. Hollister was visibly affected. She actually wiped her eyes.

"I will accept them with pleasure, Mr. Casey," she said, "but don't forget Nora is a great comfort to all of us. We have grown to love her as our own," and she opened the box thinking it might contain a pretty waist or something of that sort when to her surprise there she beheld a most magnificent set of sables. She couldn't speak. The poor woman had never dared to dream of owning such a thing. Her heart stood still and she turned and took Nora in her arms, kissing her fondly. Then she shook Mr. Casey's hand as though she would never stop.

"Mr. Casey, you are too generous. I have always loved sables, but I never expected to own a set. I don't know how to thank you for your kindness."

"Say nothing about it," replied the man. "Nora and I consider it a privilege if ye'll wear our gifts, don't we, Nora?"

"Indeed we do," replied the girl. "There are so many things that you do for me, Mrs. Hollister, that money can not compensate."

Ethel was now eighteen. One evening Harvey Bigelow invited her to the theatre. On their way home he asked her if she ever could care for him enough to become his wife.

"Oh, Harvey!" gasped Ethel, "I am so sorry. Why did you spoil our lovely friendship? I'll have to answer 'no,' and I dislike to hurt your feelings."

"That's all right, little girl," said Harvey, swallowing hard. "I was an ass to even imagine that you could care for me, but you see I'm coming on so well that I shall soon put out my sign, and I felt that you might be such a help to me; that is, if you could care for me a little bit."

"And there are so many nice girls," she said, "waiting for just such a good man as yourself."

"But, Ethel, I don't want any girl. I want one. If I can't have her I guess I'll stay single. Anyway, I suppose a man needs to practice a lot before he marries. There's a couple of years in the Hospital. But I'm glad I know the truth, Ethel. By Jove! it's off my chest. I've tried to speak of it before but I couldn't."

"I wish I could say 'yes,' Harvey; but can't we still remain the good pals that we are?"

"Why, sure," replied the man, and he took her hand. "A man needs a woman friend, don't you think?"

"Yes," replied Ethel, "and I hope to prove my friendship for you."

Ethel never spoke of her proposal, nor did Harvey; but there was a firmer bond between them than formerly.

Patty wrote often. "You never saw two people so in love as Papa and Kate. It is wonderful and remarkably right. I only feel sorry to think that through all of these years they might have been so happy, and I'm sure papa kept single for me. How selfish daughters are, Ethel; and at the same time how little they realize that they are selfish."

Ethel folded the letter and said:

"What she writes is true. You and Papa might have had all of the years of my youth to be happy in, but you sacrificed them for me, and they'll never, never come back."

"That's all right," said her mother, kissing her. "My happiness since you entered college has compensated for it, believe me, my dear little girl," and she kissed her tenderly.

CHAPTER XV

MRS. HOLLISTER ENTERTAINS

That winter Mrs. Hollister again had her teas and bridge parties, but there was no more worry about where the money was coming from; in fact, thanks to Mr. Casey's generosity she was able to pay all of her bills and put some away for a rainy day. Her little functions were delightful as usual, and the young people came in throngs to the house.

Ethel was happy in seeing her mother so contented, and in knowing that her father had no more worries. Grandmother had grown younger, and better than all, after Christmas Tom was coming to bring Aunt Susan. He had business East and he was to leave her for three weeks, after which he was to return for her.

Nora seemed less sad. She had developed into a very stylish up-to-date young woman and everyone admired and liked her.

Mrs. Hollister was in her glory. Things for her were now so comfortable and easy that she couldn't believe but what it was a dream from which she might awaken and find everything the same old way.

Mrs. Bigelow made much of Nora, taking her around and introducing her to her friends. Harvey called regularly and invited her twice a week to the theatre. He was now a young surgeon in Roosevelt Hospital on the ambulance, with a fine career open before him, and what's more he worked very hard — often until late at night. People prophesied a great future for Harvey and his parents were delighted, but none more so than Ethel, whose encouragement was genuine and like the encouragement of a sister.

Teddy Kip kept up a great correspondence with Patty, who sent him postals from every place.

"By George!" he said to the Hollisters, "do you know I correspond with three girls who are abroad and they never write letters — only postals — and if you believe it, I've got nearly a hamper filled with them — 'pon my word I have. If only Miss Patty would write a fellow a real letter once in a while I'd be grateful."

Nora received a letter from Edna Whitely.

"I have some news for all of your girls. Mollie Long and Sallie Davis are going to marry clergymen. They are brothers. Sallie's husband is going to be a missionary to China."

"Isn't that awful?" said Mrs. Hollister. "Sallie will be massacred as sure as fate—that's the end of missionaries. I had a second cousin who went and both she and her husband were victims. I wouldn't allow a child of mine to marry one. Let him stay in his own country, but to drag a young girl out into those heathen places—it's an outrage."

"Well, our Ohio Camp Fire will resolve itself into only half, I fear," said Nora. "There's poor Mattie, Miss Kate, Sallie and Mollie from right there. I wonder who's going to take their places."

"Perhaps," said Ethel, "little Mollie Hastings if she's pronounced cured.

It may be of great benefit to her. Let's see what can be done."

"Dorothy Kip might become an Ohio girl and spend her summers up there with us too," suggested Nora. "And if Dr. Bigelow goes with the Scouts Nannie can join."

"We'll see," replied Ethel. "It's quite a few months before next summer.

'Sufficient unto the day, etc.'"

Ethel was getting along famously at Barnard.

"What profession shall you follow—the law or ministry?" Harvey would ask jokingly.

"Something that shall enable me to become self supporting," Ethel would reply seriously.

"There's where you make a mistake," said Harvey. "A woman was made to be supported by a man—not to support herself."

"Why not?" asked Ethel. "How many wives today support their husbands? Have you any idea of the number?"

"Oh, well, then it's because the men are lazy or sick. No decent, self-respecting man would allow it."

"Supposing a woman can not marry. She can't propose to a man. What can she do in that case—starve? No, Dr. Bigelow, you can't even argue. Every woman should have in her hand, say, a weapon or trade with which to take care of herself. Then when the time comes she's ready to start in the battle of life, and not sit around helpless while others do for her, or become dependent upon charity, or worse. The day of Elsie Dinsmores has gone. In her place we have strong, capable, broad-minded women. Seldom do we hear of a woman fainting today, yet look back sixty years and recall the Lydia Languish females with long ringlets and wasp waists, who invariably carried smelling salts. I'm proud to belong to the women of today—healthy, strong, athletic, and brave—women who do and are not ashamed of it. Look at Aunt Susan. There's a woman who is an example. I hope I may amount to as much as she before I die."

"Ethel, I fear you are strong-minded," laughed Harvey.

"Don't fear, but know it. I try to be strong in mind and body. I believe in a woman getting all that's coming to her and working for that end."

Harvey laughed.

"Well, I shan't argue with you."

"Because you agree with me, and you know it," said Ethel quietly. "You have made yourself amount to something. Look where you were three years ago. What were your views of life then? A rich marriage. Behold the change! Now you are a man."

"Thanks," said Harvey, rising and making a low bow.

CHAPTER XVI

CHRISTMAS EVE

Christmas was near. The Hollisters wrote and invited Mr. Casey to spend the Christmas holidays with them. They also wrote Tom Harper to see if it were possible to bring Aunt Susan to be with them during the holidays. Tom replied he would make it possible. So they were to have a house full.

Nora and Ethel vied in dressing up the rooms tastefully with holly and mistletoe. Every chandelier and door had a piece of mistletoe fastened above it.

"What a grand kissing time there'll be," said Archibald. "When do we begin—on Christmas morning?"

"Now, Papa, don't you get gay," laughed Ethel. "You've led an exemplary life for fifty years. Please keep on and don't let this mistletoe make of you a different man."

Well—first came Mr. Casey. Every day he and Nora boarded a taxi and went shopping, returning with huge boxes and parcels which gradually filled Nora's closets as well as under her bed.

Then came Tom and Aunt Susan, even looking younger than before.

"Really it's ridiculous, Aunt Susan," said Ethel, "for you to keep growing so much younger and more stylish. You've got to stop."

And the bell rang so often that Mrs. Hollister was obliged to hire an extra maid for Christmas week. Everyone was so perfectly happy that it was a joy to enter the house. Harvey was there as often as his hospital practice would admit of, and he was the first to kiss Aunt Susan under the mistletoe; and Aunt Susan, if you please, now appeared in the daintiest of gowns—up-to-date and rather youthful. Ethel and Grandmother laughed over it.

"Why, Grandmother, how old is Aunt Susan?"

"She's about sixty-one," said her sister—"why?"

"Nothing, but I've been thinking wouldn't it be funny if she should marry again? She's mighty attractive in her up-to-date gowns."

"I don't see whom she could marry," said Grandmother with some asperity, "unless Mr. Casey or Dr. Bigelow." Ethel laughed.

Christmas eve arrived. They had a large tree and distributed the gifts. Everyone received exactly what he or she desired. Mr. Casey's generosity was boundless. He gave Mrs. Hollister a small limousine with the understanding that all bills should be sent to him.

"Madam," he said, "you and Nora have a great deal of shopping and social duties to perform. Nora tells me that you go by the cars and rarely in a taxi, and that you seldom allow her to pay her fare. Now this will set everything right, and Grandmother—God bless her—must have her ride daily. It is money well invested, for you and Nora can take comfort. I have engaged a good chauffeur and have made arrangements with a garage near by. All bills are to be sent to me. Nora will attend to the sending of them."

Mrs. Hollister couldn't speak. They stood under the mistletoe. She just raised herself up and gave Mr. Casey two hearty smacks, at which there arose a shout.

"I shan't try to thank you," she said, "for I can not."

Then another surprise came in shape of a wonderful diamond la valliere or pendant, and poor Mrs. Hollister was most embarrassed.

"Mr. Casey," she said, "you are going to get me in wrong. People may criticise me."

Then Tom's present came—a lovely grey silk evening wrap trimmed with chinchilla, and verily Mrs. Hollister was nearly off her head.

Grandmother received a long silk coat lined with fur and trimmed with a large lynx collar and cuffs—from Mr. Casey also.

"Don't think that I bought out a furrier," he said, "but I know people always need them."

Ethel received a lovely pendant from Mr. Casey and one from Tom, while Nora presented her with a beautiful diamond ring.

Everyone was happy this Christmas eve and strange to say Mr. Casey took Aunt Susan right under the mistletoe and kissed her, which made Grandmother laugh immoderately.

During one of the moments when people were rather quiet, Harvey Bigelow took Nora by the hand and walked up to Mr. Casey who was standing under the mistletoe; in fact, he had stood nowhere else during the evening.

"Mr. Casey," he said, "I ask of you the most valuable gift that a father can give. I ask the hand of this dear girl," and he kissed Nora gently.

Mr. Casey, who had imbibed somewhat plentifully of punch, and who was quite warm, looked at the two for a moment.

"An' is it this that ye two have been up to?" he said. "Nora, me child, do ye wish it to be?"

"Yes, Papa," faltered the girl, "I love Harvey."

"An' suppose I withhold my consent—what then?"

"Then I shall still love him, but I shall never marry without it."

"Hear that now. Nora, my good girl," and taking her hand he placed it in Harvey's, "I give her to ye. All I ask is that ye shall make her happy. Let her niver regret this day—that's all," and he wiped his eyes.

Nora flung her arms around him while Harvey wrung his hand.

"You'll never have cause to regret, nor shall she," he said. "I'll love and cherish her until death parts us, and I'll work for her so that she'll be proud of me."

Ethel kissed them both; in fact, so did everyone. Aunt Susan and Tom were delighted.

"I always liked him," she said. "Anyone who looks me square in the eye, Mr. Casey, I'll bank on every time."

It was long after midnight when the Xmas party broke up. The young man who had always played at Mrs. Hollister's teas for the sum of three dollars played the Virginia Reel, and everyone danced, — even Grandmother. Mr. Casey took so many funny fancy steps that it was hard to get him through with the figures, after which Nora and Ethel showed the elderly people how to dance the turkey trot, which of course was shocking. When the young musician left he was richer by fifty dollars — gifts of Mr. Casey, Tom Harper, and Mrs. Hollister, for she told of how lovely his mother was and how she had been her bridesmaid.

"And here's a gift for her," said Mr. Casey. "Take it and buy her a fur-lined coat," at which everyone shouted, for poor Mr. Casey's gifts had all been so comfortable and warm.

"Niver mind," he laughed, "I bet she'll like one. And give her me compliments and a Merry Christmas. And let me have your address, sir."

CHAPTER XVII

CHRISTMAS DAY

It was a typical Christmas day. There was even snow on the ground. The pretty limousine stood before the Hollisters' door and a well-groomed good-looking chauffeur was taken in and presented to Mrs. Hollister, his future mistress. Grandmother, in her handsome new cloak, and Aunt Susan with Mr. Casey, took the first ride. Mr. Casey was in high spirits over Nora's choice.

"Shure they till me that he has a great future."

"Of course he has," said Grandmother. "Why, he's advanced to the operating room and he is in line to be second assisting surgeon. Think, Mr. Casey, of the lives he may save. I think Nora has made a wise choice, and he cared for her for herself — not for her money — for he's always said that his wife's money should be settled on herself — that only the husband should pay the bills. And Nora, dear child, has improved so. She's grown so handsome and has a face full of character."

"That's so, ma'am. I would that her poor mother — God rest her soul — could but see her."

"She does," said Aunt Susan. "I firmly believe that our loved ones see us and are near us constantly. Wait a bit; I have to stop," and Mr. Casey got out at a market.

"Now what is he up to?" said Grandmother. "Susan, he's the kindest-hearted and most generous man that I ever knew."

They could catch a glimpse of him now and then. Presently he emerged with an immense basket containing a large turkey, a pair of ducks, and paper bags of vegetables, and in one corner a smaller basket of delicious fruit and a couple of wreaths. From a card he read an address to the chauffeur, who placed the Christmas basket beside him.

"Now where is he going, I wonder?" said Aunt Susan. "Perhaps some of his poor relations."

The chauffeur drove up before a cheap flat, alighted, and left the basket. Returning he nodded "yes" to Mr. Casey.

Mr. Casey said in a hesitating manner:

"The young piano player, — I thought I'd surprise him and his mother. Mrs. Hollister speaks highly of the mother and I need just such a young man with me in Columbus. I think I can find an opening for him in my office; if not, in the office of some of my friends. There are too many young men in New York; there are not enough places for them all. Now wid me they have a chance to advance, and when I'm gone they'll take my place. I've no son."

"Yes," said Grandmother, "this young musician supports his mother. My daughter-in-law says that the mother comes from a good old family. She and Mrs. Hollister were at school together in Elmira, New York state. Then when my son married Bella this lady was her bridesmaid. Bella said she was a raving beauty, but she married a man who drank himself to death, leaving her with her child alone in the world and without a penny. The boy was musical and someone taught him how to play. He used to go to school through the day and practice at night. Then he graduated and obtained a position as clerk, receiving a very moderate salary. Bella met them one night in the cars and had them come up to the house. She did all that she could for them, and employed him every time she had a tea or needed music. He played well and was glad to get his little three dollars. I know that Bella always sent home a box of refreshments to the mother."

"Well, I shall persuade them to go back wid me, and they'll have enough then, I'm thinkin'."

"Mr. Casey, you are a good man," said Aunt Susan. "The world would be better if we had more like you."

"But, Mrs. Carpenter, I think this way. The Lord has been good to me. He has caused me to prosper. Why should I consider it all me own? No, I think whenever I can help a fellow man He expects me to do so — that's all — and I try to make good."

The elderly women made no reply. He was a rough self-made man — a Roman Catholic, although not a churchman, who could give them points on charity and who did his good deeds quietly and without boasting. Mr. Casey was a Scout, although not a young one, for that was the way they were taught to do their good deeds.

Upon their arrival home he directed the chauffeur to get his dinner or luncheon and return, and after the Hollister luncheon, Nora, Harvey, Ethel and Tom went to Van Courtlandt Park, where there was skating, returning in time for six o'clock dinner.

"I think, ma'am," said Mr. Casey, "we have monopolized your car pretty well, and you never have been inside of it."

"But I'm too busy, Mr. Casey. Today is Christmas and I love to view it from the window. Just to think that it belongs to me! I can't realize it. Mr. Casey, you are my fairy Godfather and nothing else. How can I ever repay you?"

"By always being a mother to my girl, ma'am, as ye have been since she met ye. Why, ye deserve a whole garage of automobiles for the kindness ye've shown her, and see the good man she now has through ye. Don't thank me, ma'am. It's ourselves who can't thank ye enough."

CHAPTER XVIII
ANOTHER SURPRISE

After a delicious Christmas dinner the Bigelows came over. They welcomed and embraced Nora. Mrs. Bigelow really seemed sincere on this occasion. Mr. Casey liked them at once, especially Mr. Bigelow and Nannie.

"They'll make her happy all right. My girl has chosen wisely," he thought.

Tom and Ethel went out together during Christmas week. They skated and visited all the art galleries, enjoying every moment. They had many serious talks, and Ethel took Tom to call on several of her friends. The girls voted him delightful and Ethel was proud of him. They spoke of Mattie Hastings.

"Tom, Patty will never get over it," she said, "of that I'm sure."

"Ethel, don't you see, Patty witnessed it, and the shock is indelibly stamped on her memory. Time will help remove it—nothing else."

"But what a brave act, wasn't it?" continued Ethel. "Patty sends orders

for flowers once a week for her grave, and they say it looks very lovely.

And I even disliked her once. I said her eyes were too close together and

I misjudged her. Then I fairly hated Nora—think!—she who saved my life.

Each one has done something. What have I done? Whom have I benefited?

Who is better for having had me for a friend?"

They were sitting on a bench in the picture gallery of the Metropolitan Museum Ethel looked very lovely. She wore a bunch of Tom's orchids and a grey velvet suit. Her eyes were bright and her cheeks were burning red. She was visibly excited. Tom saw that she felt her life had been a failure.

"Ethel," he said, taking her hand, "think of the joy you have brought to Aunt Susan. Can't you see how much happier she is today than when you first knew her? Look at Nora. Through you she has changed from an awkward girl into a cultivated and charming woman, engaged to a fine young physician belonging to one of New York's oldest families. Indirectly you are responsible for it all. Look at little Mary Hastings. Through you she has been, or will be completely cured of her spine trouble. And lastly, look at me, Ethel, you have brought sunshine and happiness into my life. It is not always the big things that go to make happiness. It is the small things as well; and in your sweet, quiet way you have scattered light and joy in many paths. I had not intended, my dear, to speak to you of my love. I wished to wait until I had more of a name for you, and until you had come out and had a chance to choose from many men more worthy perhaps than I, but I can not keep my secret. I love you, dear, and I would have you for my wife. Can I hope? Do you care for me a little?"

Ethel's eyes shone like stars. She looked up into his face and said:

"I care for you a great deal,—until you spoke I never knew how much. If you wish I will be your wife."

Then Tom lifted her hand to his lips.

"I will make you as happy as I know how," he said. "I had a feeling that I couldn't keep my secret back after today. Come, dear, let us go and tell them all; and never under-rate yourself again."

People stared at the handsome couple and at their beaming faces. Joy was stamped on their countenances and happiness shone from their eyes.

When they arrived home, Tom walked up to Mrs. Hollister, and kissing her he said:

"I have asked Ethel to be my wife. Will you and Mr. Hollister give her to me?"

Mrs. Hollister gasped.

"Why Tom! Ethel! Is it true?"

Ethel put her arm around her mother.

"Yes, Mamma, Tom has asked me to marry him and I said 'yes,' for I know that you and Papa like him. Now you say 'yes'—do dear."

"Yes, I will say it gladly. Tom, I have always liked you and I'm sure you and Ethel will be happy. I give my consent with all my heart," and Tom took her in his arms and kissed her tenderly.

"Thank you," he said, "you have given me a precious gift. You shall never regret it."

Then they sought Mr. Hollister and were closeted with him for a long time, after which Grandmother and Aunt Susan had to be told, and lastly Nora.

So that Christmas brought two engagements in the Hollister circle.

Ethel decided to finish college before marrying, and Nora her school. The men had to be content.

"We'll have one more year at Camp anyway," said Nora. "I shall be glad to spend my last single summer there."

"And Tom and Harvey will practically be with us," said Ethel. "Nora, are you not a happy girl?"

"I am," said Nora.

"So am I," rejoined Ethel.

CHAPTER XIX

MR. CASEY BUYS A HOUSE

Aunt Susan at once began to make plans. In the meanwhile Mr. Casey asked Mr. Hollister and his mother to give him a few moments conversation on business.

"I understand that ye own this house, ma'am," he began. "What would ye sell it for?"

Mrs. Hollister looked at her son.

"Why?" she asked.

"Because I'm about to buy a house for Nora and the Doctor, and I want to buy one in this neighborhood. I also have a proposition to make to ye, Mr. Hollister. Frankly, what might be yere salary?"

Mr. Hollister reddened.

"I mean no disrespect or pryin', sir. It is a business proposition I have to make to ye, before I do to anyone else."

"My salary is three thousand a year, Mr. Casey," said Archibald Hollister. "I'm with an old and respected firm and have been with them for thirty years."

"Thin they don't value your services as they should,—pardon my sayin'. This minnit they ought to give ye more. Now I need a man like yourself to be me representative in New York. I give you the first option. Will ye come and accept the position for six thousand a year?"

Mr. Hollister acted dazed. Grandmother spoke up:

"Answer, Archibald,"

But still Archibald kept quiet.

"Is it because ye think it not honorable to leave them? Thin tell thim that I have offered ye more and see if they will do the same. I'll give you a week to see."

"And now, ma'am, I have heard that ye wished to sell. Yere Granddaughter will marry and this house will be too big for the three of yees. A pretty apartment on the Park will be far better for ye. What is yere price for the house?"

"We refused thirty thousand for it in 1900," replied Mrs. Hollister, "and real estate has increased in value since that."

"Very well," said Mr. Casey, "I know what ye say is true, and I will pay a fair price. I will give ye fifty thousand for this house, ma'am, and I will have it remodeled for my girl."

"I will accept," said Mrs. Hollister, in a prompt businesslike way.

"There is no mortgage on the house," she added.

"Yere more of a business woman than yere son. Faith, he's worryin' over hurtin' feelings of his employers I do be thinkin'," and Mr. Casey laid back and laughed.

But Archibald felt as though the earth was slowly slipping from under his feet. His luck was changing too rapidly. It was coming upon him too late in life, and Mr. Casey! Well, he was indeed the fairy Godfather. He and his wife had so longed for an apartment overlooking the Park, but Grandmother would never hear of selling.

"When I die will be time enough," she would say, and now she had actually seemed glad. And to think she would have fifty thousand dollars to live on for the rest of her life. Then this new offer from Mr. Casey, double the salary he was now receiving—it was like a dream. And his girl engaged to one of the finest men in the West. God was too good to him—he didn't deserve it.

His wife was overjoyed.

"Oh, Archie," she said "how wonderful it all is. It seems to have happened since Ethel joined the Camp Fire girls. I'm sure they have brought her luck. They have brought Nora to us and her dear father, who has been so generous, and but for the Camp Fire she never would have met Nora. Isn't it strange?"

Archibald Hollister laid the case before the Company by which he had been employed for thirty years, not telling how much his new salary was to be.

"Mr. Hollister," they said, "we can not afford to increase your salary. To be sure you have served us faithfully, but you are no longer young, and you know we need young blood in business. There are plenty waiting for your place."

That was a terrible blow to Archibald. He had not expected to get three thousand extra, but he had looked for an increase of a thousand rather than they should let him go, and to hear them calmly sit and tell him that they needed young blood was too much. He left the office, and the next morning in place of Archibald Hollister there arrived his resignation. So thirty years of faithfulness to their interests and strict attention to business didn't count with them, and there he had been so loyal to the concern!

"Ah!" said Mr. Casey, "what did I tell ye? Do ye think these corporations care for the man? No. It's for what they can get out of him — for the amount of work he can do, and for how small a salary. Let them hire their young blood and you come along with me, and we'll see how much better off they'll be!"

CHAPTER XX

ARCHIBALD'S CHANGE FOR THE BETTER

So Archibald Hollister found himself the New York manager of a large Ohio Realty Company, with four clerks under him and a couple of handsome offices; and Mr. Casey was proud of his personal appearance, for Archibald was a handsome man.

One of the clerks was the young fellow who on Christmas eve had played Money Musk for them to dance the Virginia Reel, and whose mother received on the following morning the Christmas basket from Mr. Casey.

"Now yere where ye belong," said the kind-hearted man. "I tell ye, Mr. Hollister, an honest employee should have been appreciated, and ye were not."

The family moved from the house and took a pretty apartment overlooking the Park.

They were delighted with the change and every day Ethel took long walks around the reservoir.

Mr. Casey began to renovate the interior of the house and modernize the outside.

The family lived in the limousine, and everyone seemed happy. Aunt Susan did not go home with Tom but stayed on until the family were settled in their new house. Then Tom who only wished for an excuse came on East for her. It was nearly Easter. They persuaded him to stay over, which he did.

And so here we shall leave them. After one more year there will be a double wedding, and Ethel and Nora will marry.

We see Harvey making rapid strides in his profession, and Tom building a pretty home for his Ethel, while Aunt Susan will be busy embroidering towels, napkins, etc., for their linen chest; and not only for them, but for Nora as well, for was it not through Nora and Mr. Casey that much of their happiness came?